**Christopher Hall**
**co-author and illustrator**
**Lindsey Hall**

# I DON'T WANT TO TAKE A BATH

tate publishing

CHILDREN'S DIVISION

*I Don't Want to Take a Bath*
Copyright © 2016 by Christopher Hall co-author and illustrator Lindsey Hall. All rights reserved.

This title is also available as a Tate Out Loud product. Visit www.tatepublishing.com for more information.

No part of this publication may be reproduced, stored in a retrieval system or transmitted in any way by any means, electronic, mechanical, photocopy, recording or otherwise without the prior permission of the author except as provided by USA copyright law.

The opinions expressed by the author are not necessarily those of Tate Publishing, LLC.

This novel is a work of fiction. Names, descriptions, entities, and incidents included in the story are products of the author's imagination. Any resemblance to actual persons, events, and entities is entirely coincidental.

Published by Tate Publishing & Enterprises, LLC
127 E. Trade Center Terrace | Mustang, Oklahoma 73064 USA
1.888.361.9473 | www.tatepublishing.com

Tate Publishing is committed to excellence in the publishing industry. The company reflects the philosophy established by the founders, based on Psalm 68:11,
*"The Lord gave the word and great was the company of those who published it."*

Book design copyright © 2016 by Tate Publishing, LLC. All rights reserved.
*Cover and interior design by Eileen Cueno*

Published in the United States of America

ISBN: 978-1-68254-821-9
1. Juvenile Fiction / Religious / Christian / Family
2. Juvenile Fiction / Health & Daily Living / Daily Activities
16.01.19

THIS BOOK BELONGS TO:

For Sam

Thank You to all those who have influenced and lead us in our faith journey. Kyle, thank you for your inspiration and clever ideas.

It was bath time, and Eric was not interested in a bath. "Daddy," he said, "I'm pretty sure the Bible says I don't have to take a bath."

"What? Where does it say that?" asked his surprised father.

As the tub began to fill, Eric said, "Noah was about to get the biggest bath of all time." (Gen. 6:17)

"And God helped him build an ark to save him from the bath." (Gen. 7)

"God promised never to send a terrible bath again." To help his father understand, Eric pulled the plug and smiled as the water swirled down the drain. (Gen. 9:12–17)

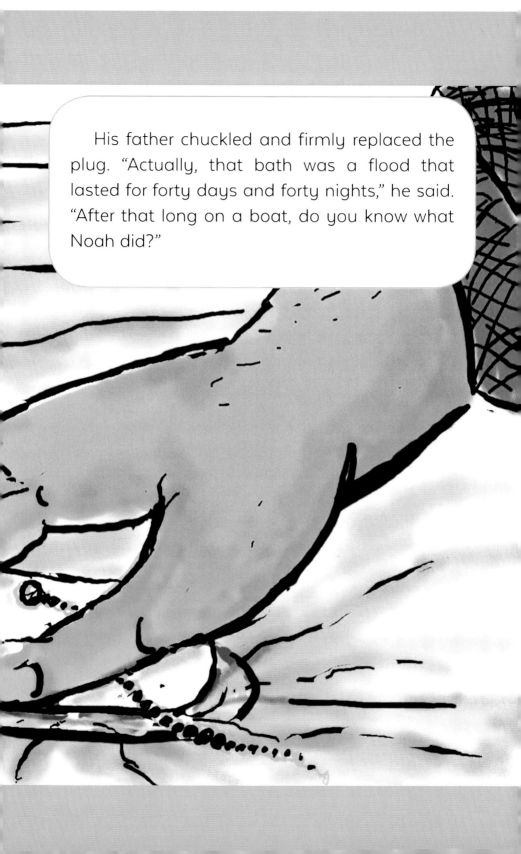

His father chuckled and firmly replaced the plug. "Actually, that bath was a flood that lasted for forty days and forty nights," he said. "After that long on a boat, do you know what Noah did?"

"Noah took a bath," said Eric's father, and he started adding bubbles to the tub.

But Eric wasn't ready to give up yet. "Wait!" he said.

Eric tried again, "When Moses was leading his friends to the promised land, some bad guys wanted to give them all a bath." (Exod. 14:5–12)

"But God parted the waters so Moses and his friends wouldn't have to take a bath." (Exod. 14:13-21)

"And gave the bad guys a bath instead!" Eric's story even soaked his father. (Exod. 14:21–28)

Eric's father dried off and said, "The friends still had to walk through the desert for forty years. Do you know what they needed after that?" (Exod. 16, Exod. 17:5-7)

"A bath," sighed Eric, and then he quickly tried one last time, "But wait! Jesus didn't need a bath."

"He'd walk on water instead!" (Mt. 14:22–33)

Eric's dad started to fill a cup. "Actually, Jesus had the most important bath of all time."

As he rinsed his son's hair, Eric's father explained, "When Jesus was baptized, He took a bath in the Jordan River. He was washed with water and the Holy Spirit so He and everyone knew that His life was committed to God, His Father." (Mt. 3:13–16)

Eric got out of the bath, and his dad toweled him off. As Eric snuggled under the warm towel, his dad said, "And after Jesus took His bath, His Father said..."

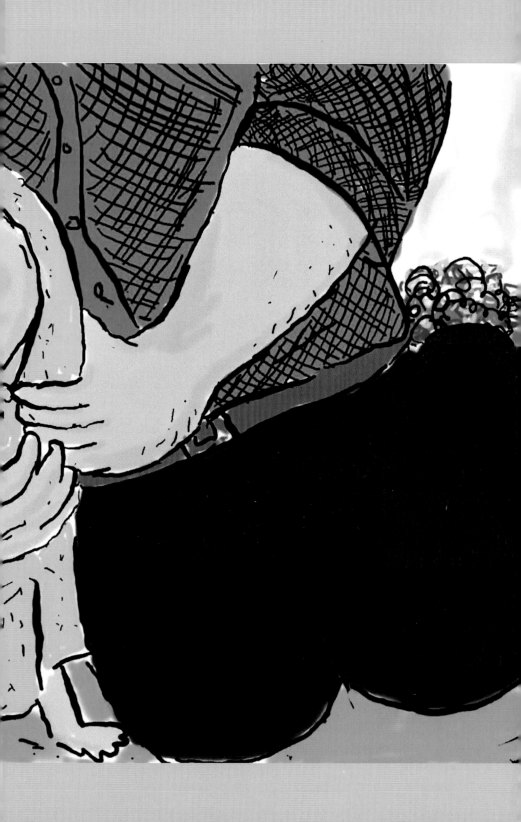

"This is my Son with whom I am well pleased."
(Mt. 3:17)

# listen|imagine|view|experience

## AUDIO BOOK DOWNLOAD INCLUDED WITH THIS BOOK!

In your hands you hold a complete digital entertainment package. In addition to the paper version, you receive a free download of the audio version of this book. Simply use the code listed below when visiting our website. Once downloaded to your computer, you can listen to the book through your computer's speakers, burn it to an audio CD or save the file to your portable music device (such as Apple's popular iPod) and listen on the go!

How to get your free audio book digital download:

1. Visit www.tatepublishing.com and click on the e|LIVE logo on the home page.
2. Enter the following coupon code:
   4db1-3496-b022-009c-0221-efe4-b2e2-19bb
3. Download the audio book from your e|LIVE digital locker and begin enjoying your new digital entertainment package today!